W9-DFK-619

This book is dedicated to all
who have been treated as,
or felt different than, the rest.

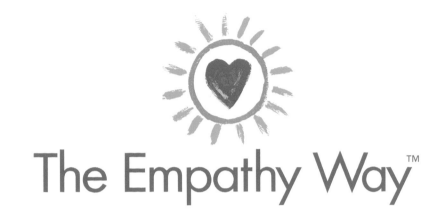

The Empathy Way™

I'm Different You're Different

by Anne Paris

photography by Marian Brickner

Hi! I'm Jenga. I'm a bonobo. I want to tell you a story about me and my new friend, Kaleb.

I'll start my story before I knew Kaleb. I'm a happy kind of boy. I've got a mom and dad who love me, and we have lots of fun playing and hanging out together.

I want to be just like Dad when I grow up. He tries to understand how I feel. He calls it empathy.

So I try to understand how my friends feel too. Sometimes I THINK I know what Laney feels, but when I ask her I find out I was wrong. So then she tells me how she really feels. That's empathy!

Laney and I feel best when we really understand how each other feels. We have lots of friends. Some would say I am popular. Me? I just like to be happy, play games, and be nice to others.

One day a new kid moved in. His name was Kaleb. Some of his hair was missing. To tell you the truth, I thought he looked kind of weird. I thought he WAS weird.

I thought something was wrong with him. He looked SO different.

Laney and I didn't want to play with him. He was bald and had big ears.

Laney looked closely at Kaleb, and then whispered to me,
"He looks DIFFERENT…let's get away from him!"

So Laney and I ran away from Kaleb.

Kaleb ran to his mom to be held.
He felt sad.

Then I remembered empathy. I started to wonder how Kaleb felt. I was worried that Kaleb felt sad and alone because we didn't want to play with him. So I talked to my mom about it.

I told her, "Laney and I ran away from Kaleb because he looks so different. But now I'm worried because he looks so sad."

My mom said, "I understand it's scary when someone looks different than you. You don't know if he is different on the inside, too."

My mom got it! My feelings made sense.

"Right," I said, "but I'm also good at empathy and don't want Kaleb to feel sad…so I think I am going to talk to him."

"I'm so proud of you," my mom said, "no wonder you have so many friends!" I was proud of myself, too.

Later that day, I was sitting with my mom and Kaleb walked by. All of a sudden, I felt nervous again. "He looks so DIFFERENT," I thought to myself. "Do I really want to be friends with him? Maybe he IS weird."

"What will my friends think of me if I talk to him? Will they think I'm weird, too?" I wasn't sure what to do. My mom gently urged me to say "hi" to him.

"The empathy way is the best," I said to myself, and sat down beside Kaleb.

"Hi, Kaleb, my name is Jenga." Kaleb was quiet. I think he expected me to make fun of him. "Would you like to play?"

Kaleb smiled and said, "Yes! Other kids don't want to play with me because I look different. But I can't help it. You see, I don't have much hair because my mommy loves me SO much."

"What?" I didn't expect to hear that! "What do you mean, your mommy loves you SO much?" I asked.

"My mommy and I like to laugh and cuddle and have fun. She is the best mommy but…

She goes a little overboard when she is grooming me. She makes sure I'm always clean, but she is so careful, and cleans me so much, that some of my hair has fallen out."

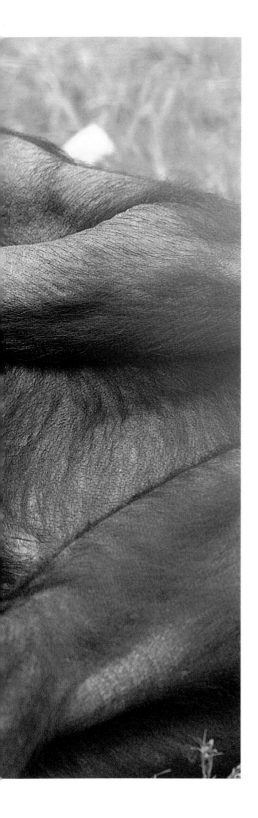

"It's ok, though. I love her and she loves me. She cleans herself the same way—A LOT—her hair is thin, too!"

"Wow!" I said. "I never knew that!"

So Kaleb isn't weird or different at all. He is just over-loved!

I was starting to like this kid. So we started playing.

We played chase!

I found out he was fun and he could do tricks!

28

When Laney and Lucy saw how much fun we were having, they decided to play with us too!

We all became good friends, just like a gang of superheroes!

Kaleb even taught us how to do some cool new stunts on the ropes. I'm so glad I knew about empathy and got to know him.

Once Kaleb felt like we understood him, he showed us how funny he was! He put on a big shirt and joked, "I am who I am—I've just got to be me!" He made us all giggle.

And now, instead of seeing him as weird and different, we all think he is funny and kind of cute!

We feel happy now that we're all friends.

And now Kaleb is one happy,
over-loved, and understood bonobo.
And thanks to the empathy way we
all feel connected.

How do you decide who is different?

Children, please discuss this with your class, teacher, parents, and friends.

Dear Adult,

Social rejection and alienation is a painful reality for many children and can lead to depression, behavior problems, and even suicide. Facilitating empathy in our children can help them to deal with this problem.

As parents and educators, we must increase our own empathy, not only with the rejected children, but also with the "rejecters."

People avoid "different" others because they fear rejection by their friends if they accept the odd one, and because they fear what lies beneath an unfamiliar, different exterior. If we understand, rather than judge, these fears, our empathy will help children move beyond their fears and doubts.

Bonobos are wonderful teachers of healthy social behavior because they seem to have figured it out. Bonobos are known for their peaceful communities, their readiness to work out disagreements and make up with each other, and for their compassionate and empathetic behaviors within the group.

Although the story line in this book is fictional, the photographs clearly display the emotional connections between the individual bonobos. All of the photographs are of a community of bonobos who live at the Jacksonville Zoo and Gardens in Jacksonville, Florida.

Anne Wessels-Paris, PhD

ABOUT THE AUTHOR AND PHOTOGRAPHER

Anne Wessels-Paris, PhD is a Clinical Psychologist and empathy expert. She is in private practice in Cincinnati, Ohio, and works with individuals and families. She is author of the grown-up book, **Standing at Water's Edge: Moving Past Fear, Blocks, and Pitfalls to Discover the Power of Creative Immersion** (2008, New World Library). Dr. Paris can be reached at anne@anneparis.com or her website, AnneParis.com

Marian Brickner is a whimsical animal photographer. She has images published in: **I'm Lucy: A Day in the Life of a Young Bonobo**, afterword by Jane Goodall. Cover of **The Bonobo and the Atheist** by Frans de Waal. **Animals Don't Wear Lipstick, Growing Up Bonobo, What Are They Thinking?, Paws on a Line, (Claws and Hoofs Too), Seasoned Dogs, Mutts and Rascals, Tale of Dales, With Bright Shiny Faces, What's a Family Anyway,** and more. Marian can be reached at insect1@att.net or her website at MarianBricknerPhotography.com